HAMILTON'S HATS

First published 1996 as *Juice the Pig* by Macmillan Children's Books
Published 2007 as *Hamilton's Hats* by Macmillan Children's Books
This edition published 2008 by Macmillan Children's Books
a division of Macmillan Publishers Limited
20 New Wharf Road, London N1 9RR
Basingstoke and Oxford
Associated companies throughout the world
www.panmacmillan.com

ISBN: 978-0-230-01481-7

11 13 15 14 12 10

A CIP catalogue record for this book is available from the British Library.

Printed in China

HAMILTON'S HATS

Martine Oborne

Illustrated by Axel Scheffler

MACMILLAN CHILDREN'S BOOKS

Hamilton the Pig was very fond of hats. He had . . .

big hats,   small hats,   tall hats,

floppy hats,   stripy hats,   feathery hats,

and suitable-for-every-and-any-occasion sort of hats.

In fact, he had so many hats that you would need more than all your fingers and toes to count them.

When Hamilton the Pig's mum saw Hamilton messing about in his hats, she worried.

"Hamilton," she would say, "you are a very vain little pig and I do not know what is to become of you. You have many lessons to learn in life and you will learn none of them from hats!"

But Hamilton did not listen. He was too busy

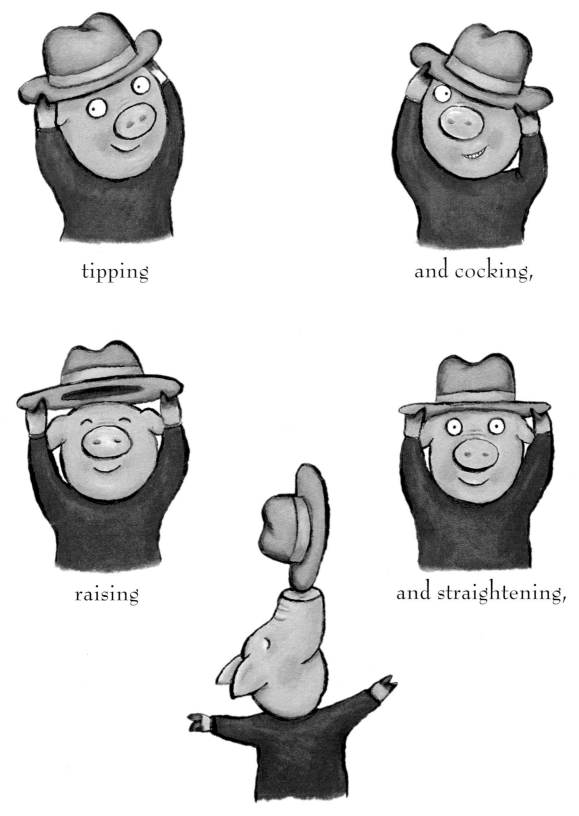

tipping

and cocking,

raising

and straightening,

and doing all the other things you do with hats.

One day, Hamilton the Pig was out and about when he bumped into a giraffe. Hamilton was wearing a tall, teetering, high-as-a-chimney sort of hat. "My hat makes me almost as tall as you!" he said to the giraffe.

The giraffe snorted and with one fell swooooop

snatched up the hat   and flipped it onto her head.

"Mmmmm, indeed, a very fine hat," she said, ignoring the hot, cross piglet below. "I should like to keep it for myself."

"But if you are really determined to get your hat back, you must climb up my long, long neck to get it."

Hamilton looked up at the giraffe's long, long legs and her long, long neck.

It is not easy for little pigs to climb, but Hamilton did want his hat back and so he decided to do it.

It was horrid. The giraffe kept wriggling her neck because, she said, Hamilton was so tickly.

But Hamilton was determined and so, at last, he got his hat.

"Wheeeee!"

he cried as he slid down the back of the giraffe's neck and bomped onto the ground. "I am a very determined pig and I have my hat!"

The next day, Hamilton the Pig was out and about when he came across a crocodile.

Hamilton was wearing a fierce, pointy, snap-your-tail-off sort of hat. "My hat makes me almost as fierce as you!" he said to the crocodile.

The crocodile yawned

and, with a quick slurpety-slurp,

schnaffled the hat deep inside his mouth.

"Mmmmm, indeed, a very gobblesome hat. I should like to eat it for my dinner," drooled the crocodile, ignoring the raging pink piglet. "But if you are really brave enough to get your hat back, you must come inside my hungry, hungry jaws to get it."

Hamilton looked at the crocodile's hungry, hungry jaws and his hungry, hungry smile.

It is not easy for little pigs to jump inside a crocodile's mouth, but Hamilton did want his hat back and so he decided to do it.

It was terrifying. The crocodile kept licking his lips because, he said, Hamilton was so tasty. But Hamilton was brave and so, at last, he got his hat.

"Hurrah!" he shouted as he leapt off the crocodile's tongue and ran off as fast as he could. "I am a very determined and brave pig and I have my hat!"

The next day, Hamilton the Pig was out and about when he met a band of monkeys.

Hamilton was wearing a round, bouncy, let's-play-catch sort of hat. "My hat makes me almost as playful as you!" he said to the band of monkeys.

The monkeys laughed and, with a quick flick of the tail,

one monkey swiped the hat and threw it to his friend.

"Mmmmm, indeed, a very fun hat. We should play with it every day,"
cried the monkeys, ignoring the angry piggy in the middle.

"But, if you are patient, you can have it back when we are finished."
Hamilton watched the monkeys throw his hat high, high into the air. It is not easy for little pigs to be patient, but Hamilton did want his hat back and so he decided to do it.

Poor Hamilton. It was boring.

The monkeys played for hours because, they said, it was such fun teasing Hamilton.

But Hamilton was patient and so, in the end, he got his hat.

"At last!" he sighed as he said goodbye
to the monkeys and plodded off.
"I am a very determined, brave and
patient pig and I have my hat!"

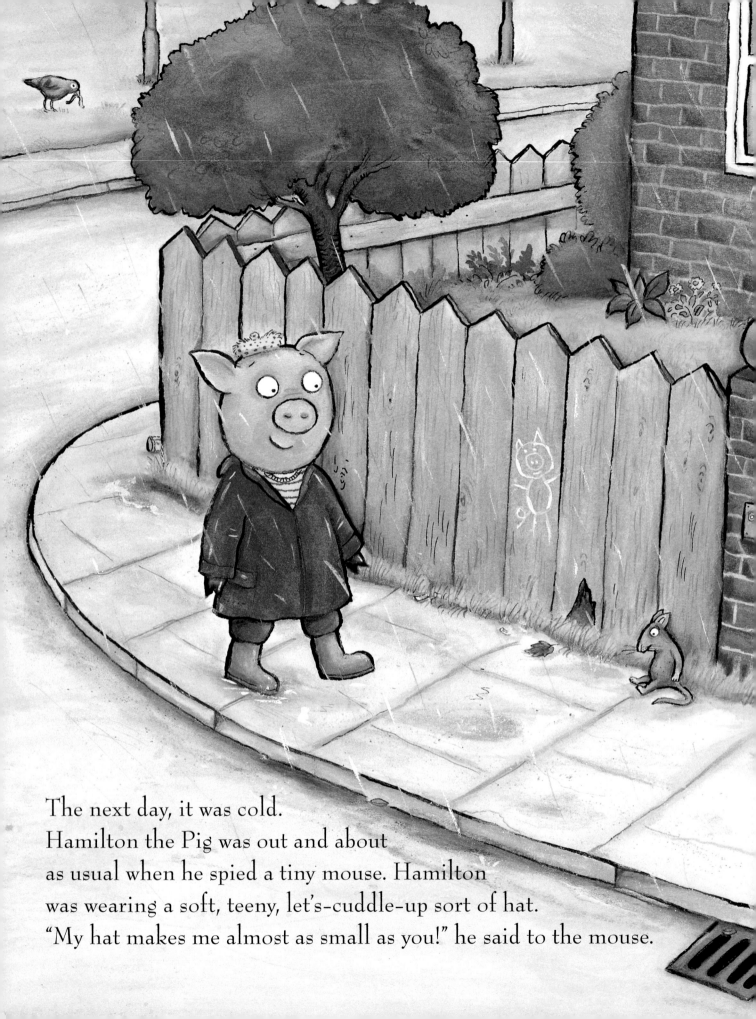

The next day, it was cold.
Hamilton the Pig was out and about
as usual when he spied a tiny mouse. Hamilton
was wearing a soft, teeny, let's-cuddle-up sort of hat.
"My hat makes me almost as small as you!" he said to the mouse.

The tiny mouse sniffed and looked up at the hat.
A slow, miserable tear rolled down her cheek.

"What's the matter?" asked Hamilton.

"I'm cold and I have no house to live in. Your hat looks so cuddly and warm. It would be just the thing to curl up inside on a winter's night."

"You want to sleep in my hat?" squealed Hamilton, horrified.

"Oh no," said the tiny mouse, "I could not possibly ask you to be so kind as to give me your hat."

Hamilton looked at the mouse as she limped unhappily away. It is not easy for little pigs to be generous and Hamilton did not want to give his hat away, but he decided to do it.

It was nice. The mouse kept shaking his hand and saying thank you because, she said, Hamilton was so kind.

"Ah," said Hamilton, "I am a very determined, brave, patient and kind pig but I have no hat!"

So, happy, hungry and hatless, Hamilton the Pig arrived home . . .

and set to work on a new and very special hat!